It's fun to draw
Fairies
and
Mermaids

Mark Bergin

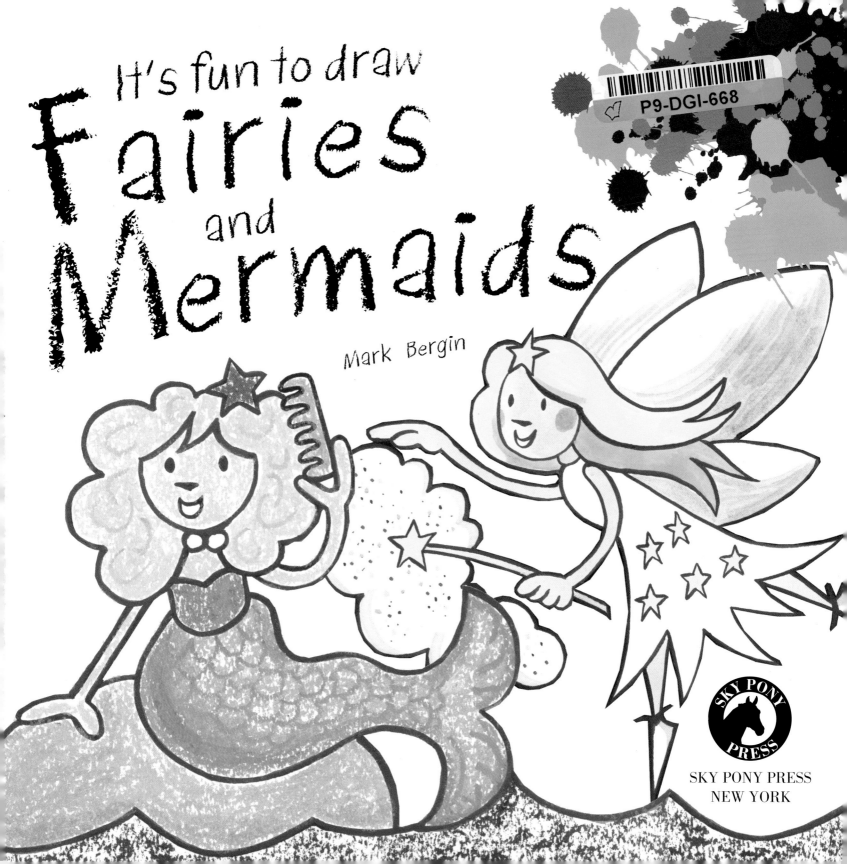

SKY PONY PRESS
NEW YORK

Mark Bergin was born in Hastings, England. He has illustrated an award-winning series and written over twenty books. He has done many book designs, layouts, and storyboards in many styles including cartoon for numerous books, posters, and advertisements. He lives in Bexhill-on-sea with his wife and three children.

HOW TO USE THIS BOOK:

Start by following the numbered splats on the left-hand page. These steps will ask you to add some lines to your drawing. The new lines are always drawn in red so you can see how the drawing builds from step to step. Read the "You can do it!" splats to learn about drawing and coloring techniques you can use.

Copyright © 2013 by Mark Bergin
First published by The Salariya Book Company Ltd,
© The Salariya Book Company Limited 2012

Sky Pony Press books may be purchased in bulk at special discounts for sales promotion, corporate gifts, fund-raising, or educational purposes. Special editions can also be created to specifications. For details, contact the Special Sales Department, Sky Pony Press, 307 West 36th Street, 11th Floor, New York, NY 10018 or info@skyhorsepublishing.com.

Sky Pony® is a registered trademark of Skyhorse Publishing, Inc.®, a Delaware corporation.

Visit our website at www.skyponypress.com.

10 9 8 7 6 5

Manufactured in China, April 2015
This product conforms to CPSIA 2008

Library of Congress Cataloging-in-Publication Data

Bergin, Mark, 1961-
It's fun to draw fairies and mermaids / Mark Bergin.
pages cm
Includes index.
ISBN 978-1-62087-112-6 (pbk. : alk. paper) 1. Fairies in art--Juvenile literature. 2. Mermaids in art--Juvenile literature. 3. Drawing--Technique--Juvenile literature. I. Title.
NC825.F22B47 2013
743'.87--dc23
                                          2012038261

Contents

Coral, a mermaid

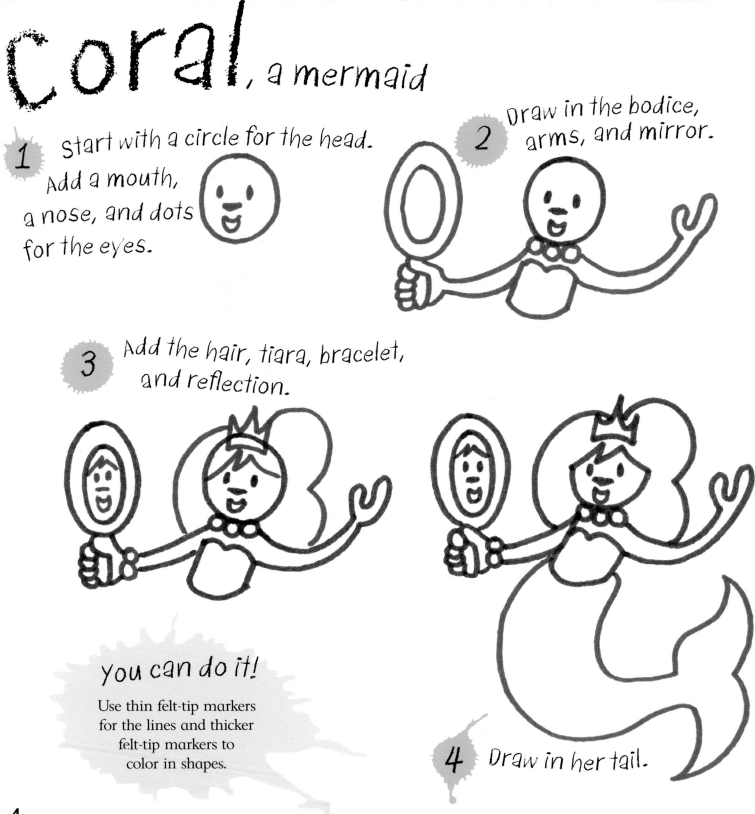

1 Start with a circle for the head. Add a mouth, a nose, and dots for the eyes.

2 Draw in the bodice, arms, and mirror.

3 Add the hair, tiara, bracelet, and reflection.

you can do it!

Use thin felt-tip markers for the lines and thicker felt-tip markers to color in shapes.

4 Draw in her tail.

5

Buttercup, a fairy

1 Start with the head. Add a nose, a mouth, and dots for eyes.

2 Draw in the dress.

you can do it!

Use a felt-tip marker for the lines. Add color with oil pastels. Use your finger to smudge the colors.

Splat-a-fact!

Woodland fairies look after the flowers and trees, with the help of the small creatures who live there.

3 Add the arms and legs.

4 Draw in two wings and her hair.

6

Pearl, a mermaid

1 Start with the head, the mouth, and a a dot for the eye.

Splat-a-fact!
Mermaids and mermen have lived in the ocean since the beginning of time.

2 Add the hair and tiara.

3 Draw in the bodice and arms.

4 Add her tail.

5 Finish the drawing, adding a crab and rock.

sparkle, the Tooth Fairy

1 Start with the head. Add a mouth, a nose, and dots for the eyes.

2 Add the hair.

3 Draw in the dress.

you can do it!
Use a felt-tip marker for the outline. Add color using crayons.

4 Add the arms and legs.

Splat-a-fact!
The tooth fairy collects children's baby teeth and leaves a gift in return.

5 Draw in wings, a wand, and a bow in the hair.

sandy, a mermaid

1 Cut out the head. Add a mouth and eye and glue them down.

you can do it!
Cut out the shapes from colored paper. Glue these onto to a sheet of blue paper. Use a felt-tip marker for the lines.

2 Cut out the hair. Glue down.

MAKE SURE YOU GET AN ADULT TO HELP YOU WHEN USING SCISSORS!

3 Cut out the arms and chest. Glue down.

4 Cut out a long green tail, a flower, and some beads. Glue down.

Splat-a-fact!
Mermaids often come to the rescue of shipwrecked sailors.

13

Bubbles, a mermaid

1 Start with the head. Add the nose, mouth, and dots for the eyes.

2 Draw in the body and tail.

you can do it!
Use a felt-tip marker for the outlines. Scribble the colors with various colored oil pastels.

3 Add the hair, necklace, and bikini top.

4 Add the arms and hands.

14

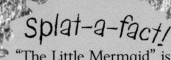

Poppy, the Flower Fairy

1 Start with the head. Add a nose, a mouth, and dots for the eyes.

2 Add the dress.

you can do it!

Use a graphite stick for the lines. Add ink washes. Sponge inks on or add a second colored ink on top of an area that is still wet for extra effects.

Splat-a-fact!

There are fairies all around us, but they are so small that only children can see them.

3 Draw in the arms and legs.

4 Add hair, wings, and a collar.

Princess Oceana

1 Start with the head. Add the mouth and two dots for the eyes.

you can do it!

Use crayons for texture and paint over it with watercolor paint. Use a felt-tip marker for the lines.

2 Add the body, bikini top, and beads.

3 Draw in the hair and a crown.

4 Draw the long, curved tail.

5 Add the arms.

splat-a-fact!
Mermaids keep
their tails shiny by
rubbing them daily
with seaweed.

19

Melody, a mermaid

1 Start with the head. Add a nose, a mouth, and two dots for the eyes.

2 Add her hair.

you can do it!
Draw the outline with a felt-tip marker and color it in with pastel pencils.

Splat-a-fact!
Mermaids can live for 300 years.

3 Add the bodice and beads.

4 Draw in the arms and hands holding a harp with four strings.

5 Add the tail and a rock.

The Fairy Princess

1 Cut out the wings. Glue down.

you can do it!

Cut out shapes from colored paper. Glue them onto a sheet of paper as shown. Use a felt-tip marker for the face.

2 Cut out the hair and a dress. Glue down.

3 Cut out the head and arms. Glue down. Add a nose, a mouth, and eyes with a felt-tip marker.

4 Cut out a crown, the legs, and shoes. Glue down.

23

Splat-a-fact!
A "fairy ring" is a circle of toadstools where the fairies gather to dance.

MAKE SURE
YOU GET AN
ADULT TO HELP
YOU WHEN
USING SCISSORS!

Holly, the Christmas Fairy

1 Start with an oval for the head. Add eyes, a nose, and a mouth.

you can do it!

Use crayons for texture and paint over it with watercolor paint. Use a felt-tip marker for the lines.

2 Add the shape of the hair.

3 Draw the body and dress.

4 Add arms holding a present.

5 Draw the legs and feet.

6 Add bows to the hair and present.

7 Finish by adding the wings.

24

Splat-a-fact!

Titania, Queen of the fairies, lives in a fairy castle with her husband, King Oberon.

25

Pebbles, a mermaid

1 Start with the head. Add a nose, a mouth, and dots for eyes.

you can do it!
Use a felt-tip marker for the lines. Add color using chalky pastels. Use your fingers to blend the colors.

2 Add the hair and beads.

Splat-a-fact!
Mermaids are beautiful creatures that are half human and half fish.

3 Draw in the bodice and tail.

4 Add the arms and the rock.

5 Draw in her hair clip and comb.

Twinkle, a fairy

1 Start with the head. Add the nose, mouth, and dots for the eyes.

2 Draw in the neck and hair.

3 Add the dress.

you can do it!
Use markers to fill in the background and to add color details. Use a felt-tip marker for the lines.

Splat-a-fact!
A fairy always carries a pinch of magic dust to help with her spells.

4 Draw in arms and legs.

5 Add a wand and wings.

Ella, the Dust Fairy

1 Start with the head. Add a mouth, a nose, and two dots for the eyes.

2 Add the dress.

3 Draw in the hair and arms.

you can do it!

Use crayons to create patterns and texture. Paint over it with watercolor paints. Use a felt-tip marker for the lines.

4 Draw in the feather and the legs.

5 Add two wings.

Index

Splat-a-fact!

Not all fairies have wings. Some fairies don't fly at all.